Have fun on your a
Nana and Itty Bitty !!

Victoria Martin

This book is dedicated to the real
Itty Bitty, a very lovable and slobbery
143-pound Newfoundland dog.

-Victoria

www.mascotbooks.com

Itty Bitty Wouldn't Budge

©2015 Victoria Martin. All Rights Reserved. No part of this publication may be reproduced, stored in a retrieval system or transmitted in any form by any means electronic, mechanical, or photocopying, recording or otherwise without the permission of the author.

For more information, please contact:
Mascot Books
560 Herndon Parkway #120
Herndon, VA 20170
info@mascotbooks.com

Library of Congress Control Number: 2014920242

CPSIA Code: PRT0115A
ISBN-13: 978-1-62086-828-7

Printed in the United States

Itty Bitty
Wouldn't Budge

Written by
Victoria Martin

Illustrated by
Caitlyn Knepka

Itty Bitty, a beautiful and very large
Newfoundland dog, lived with her owner, Nana,
in a wonderful little town called Maplewood.
Itty Bitty was as big as a small pony!

Nana was a beloved elementary
school teacher.

Everyone in town knew Nana.
Everyone in town knew Itty Bitty.

It was a beautiful, sunny and warm spring day.
Itty Bitty and Nana decided to go for a walk.

They went down the steps of their house, past the church on the corner, through the park, behind the railroad station, and all around the little village.

They stopped along the way to talk to friends and shopkeepers.

It was getting close to sunset and time
to walk back home.

They stopped at a crosswalk and waited
for the light to turn green.

Itty Bitty settled on the grass.

The light changed and it was time
to cross the street.

Nana gently tugged at Itty Bitty's leash...
But Itty Bitty wouldn't budge.

Nana used gentle words to persuade her
to move...But Itty Bitty wouldn't budge.

The town's fire truck passed by and stopped. The captain asked Nana if she needed any help.

Nana replied, "Hello, Captain. Thank you for your offer but we are just enjoying this beautiful, sunny and warm spring day."

A police car came by and stopped. The officer asked Nana if she needed any help. Nana replied, "Hello, Officer. Thank you for your offer but we are just enjoying this beautiful, sunny and warm spring day."

Many of Nana's students and their parents passed by as well. Nana smiled and waved. She said out loud, "Hello! Isn't this a beautiful, sunny and warm spring day?"

Even though Nana was smiling and waving, she was getting worried. The sun was beginning to set and they really needed to get home.

Nana had an idea.

She said to Itty Bitty,
"You have a big carrot waiting for
you at home. You love carrots."

Itty Bitty thought about this – she did love
her carrots. But Itty Bitty wouldn't budge.

Then Nana said, "I'll bet your stuffed animal, Duck, is missing you right now. It is your favorite toy."

Itty Bitty thought about this too. She was completely in love with Duck. But still, Itty Bitty wouldn't budge.

Finally, Nana said, "If we go home now and you eat all of your dinner, you can have vanilla ice cream."

Itty Bitty's ears perked up! Nana reminded her about her special ice cream treat that was waiting for her every night after dinner.

Yes, of course! Itty Bitty loved her after-dinner treat more than anything—definitely more than carrots—and maybe...just maybe...more than Duck.

Itty Bitty eased herself up, stretched her paws and her tail, and was ready to walk home.

Nana was very relieved.

Off they went and before the sun set, they were home for dinner and an ice cream treat.

Then Itty Bitty took Duck, curled up on her bed, and went to sleep.

Goodnight...Sleep tight!

The End

Photo credit to Leslie Lerman

About the Author

Victoria Martin and her family have been the proud and happy owners of many dogs of every mixed breed for as long as she can remember. Nana and Itty Bitty hold a very special place in her heart and this book is a tribute to them. In support of dogs and their best friends everywhere, a portion of the author's proceeds from the sale of this book will be donated to the Best Friends Animal Society.

Thank you to all of my family and friends for being very understanding and very supportive of my late-blooming creative writing endeavors.

Thank you to Linda Eglinton for being at the right place at the right time to give me the incentive to write this wonderfully true story.

Thank you to Leslie Lerman for her unbridled enthusiasm and for being there when I signed on the dotted line.